the king's
choice

A
FOLKTALE FROM INDIA

Retold by K. SHIVKUMAR

# The king's choice

Illustrated by YOKO MITSUHASHI

PARENTS' MAGAZINE PRESS
NEW YORK

Typographic Design: Kei Kubo

Text copyright © 1961 by Children's Book Trust, New Delhi, India
Illustrations copyright © 1971 by Yoko Mitsuhashi
All rights reserved. Printed in the United States of America
ISBN: Trade 0-8193-0364-X, Library 0-8193-0365-8
Library of Congress Catalog Card Number: 76-81195

**T**here
was once a lion
who was king of the forest.
He was big and strong.
He was both handsome
and fierce.

**A**ll the other animals
in the forest called him king and
brought him gifts from every
corner of the land.
But the more the lion had,
the more he wanted.

"A king
must have a court,"
he said to himself
one day.

The lion called a fox to his side. "You are known to be a wise and clever creature, Fox," said the lion. "I want you to be my adviser."

"Thank you, Your Majesty," said the fox, bowing low.

The lion next called a leopard to his side. "You are known to be watchful and swift of foot, Leopard. I want you to be my bodyguard," said the lion.

"Thank you, Your Majesty," said the leopard, bowing low.

The lion then called a vulture to his side.
"You are a bird, Vulture, and can fly high,"
the lion said. "You will be my messenger."
"Thank you, Your Majesty," said the vulture, bowing low.

T he fox, the vulture, and the leopard took an oath of
loyalty to the king. The king promised to meet them as
friends and to give them food and protection. For some time
all went well in the lion king's court. The three courtiers never
opposed the king. His wishes were law. Whenever he roared,
they came running. Whenever he took a walk, they meekly followed
behind him. When the lion king went hunting, they found the
animals for him to kill. And after he had had
his meal, he left the remains for them.

So they always
had enough
to eat.

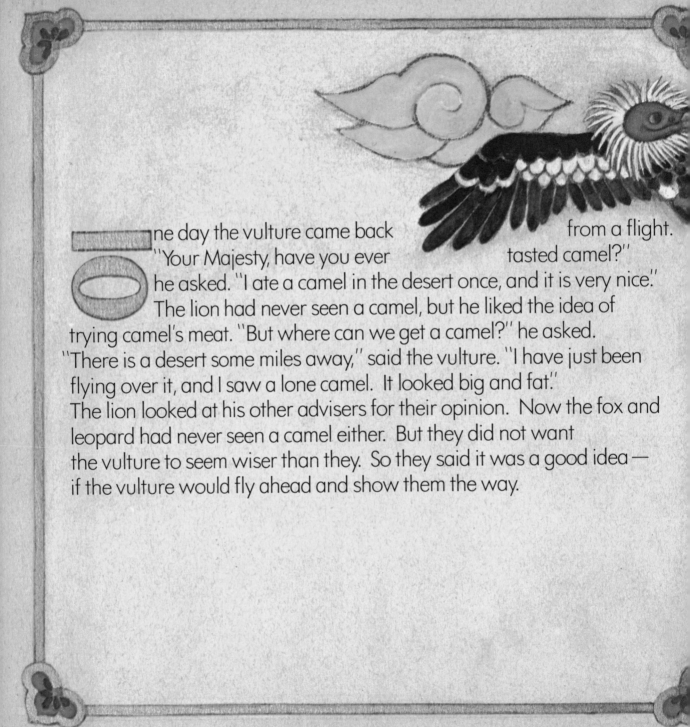

ne day the vulture came back from a flight. "Your Majesty, have you ever tasted camel?" he asked. "I ate a camel in the desert once, and it is very nice." The lion had never seen a camel, but he liked the idea of trying camel's meat. "But where can we get a camel?" he asked. "There is a desert some miles away," said the vulture. "I have just been flying over it, and I saw a lone camel. It looked big and fat." The lion looked at his other advisers for their opinion. Now the fox and leopard had never seen a camel either. But they did not want the vulture to seem wiser than they. So they said it was a good idea — if the vulture would fly ahead and show them the way.

So the vulture's idea was approved. And the next morning the lion and his court started off on the camel hunt. They reached the edge of the desert easily. But after they had left the shelter of the forest, the day became very hot. The sun shone down with fire-hot rays.

The vulture flew high up in the cooler air.
"Hurry along," he called. "The camel is not far off."
But the lion could not hurry anymore.
The hot sand had burned his paws.

"**S**top!" he shouted to the others. "I can walk no farther. Let us go back to the forest. I do not care to try camel meat." The lion king's advisers were frightened. The forest was far behind them. They did not know how to get the lion back home. The leopard wanted to run away. The vulture wanted to watch and wait and eat the lion later on. But the clever fox thought of a plan. Off into the desert he ran, saying, "I will soon bring help."

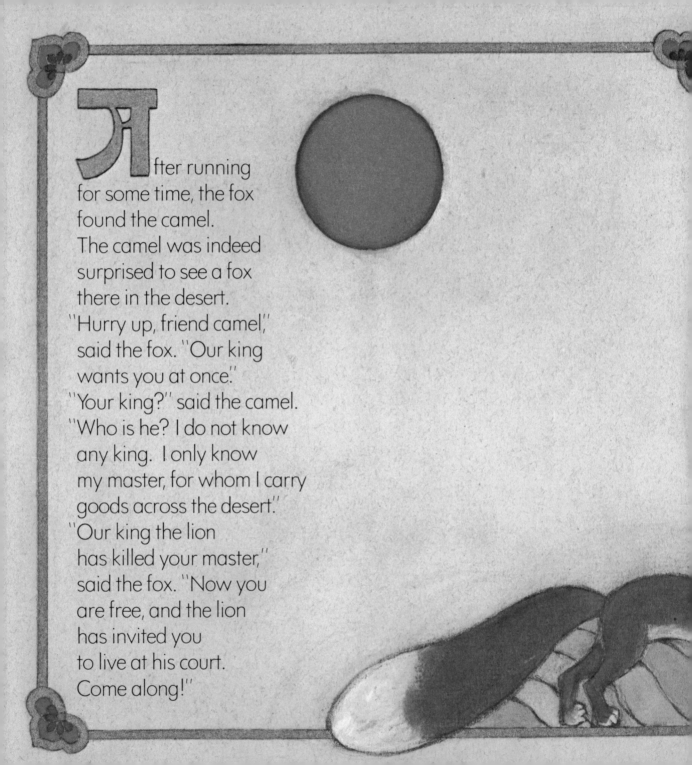

**A**fter running
for some time, the fox
found the camel.
The camel was indeed
surprised to see a fox
there in the desert.
"Hurry up, friend camel,"
said the fox. "Our king
wants you at once."
"Your king?" said the camel.
"Who is he? I do not know
any king. I only know
my master, for whom I carry
goods across the desert."
"Our king the lion
has killed your master,"
said the fox. "Now you
are free, and the lion
has invited you
to live at his court.
Come along!"

To the camel followed the fox. When the fox and the camel reached the lion's camp, the vulture and the leopard were surprised. The lion looked pleased, in spite of his burned paws. The camel was presented to the king and agreed to serve the lion in return for a home at his court. "Get on the camel's back, Your Majesty," said the fox. "We will return home."

ऊ he lion at once jumped on-
to the camel's back. His courtiers,
the fox and the leopard, jumped
up behind him. And with the
vulture flying ahead as a guide,
they set off on the long journey
back to the forest.

hen the travelers again reached the king's domain, they were all very tired and hungry after a long day. The fox and the leopard and the vulture looked at the camel. Then they looked at one another and smiled hungry smiles. They had brought the camel for the king's dinner. Now it was time for the feast! The lion king knew what his courtiers were thinking. He called the camel to him.

"**F**riend camel," he said, "I have to thank you for saving my life. You are welcome to live at my court as long as you wish. I promise you my protection." This did not please the courtiers a bit. Had they not risked their lives so that he could try camel meat? And now the king wanted to let the camel live. But they could do nothing. After all, the king was the king. So they waited. Now the lion's paws were so badly burned that he did not feel like going hunting. But that did not keep him from being very hungry indeed. "Fox! Leopard! Vulture!" he shouted. "Don't you see that I am ill and hungry? Go and get me some food!"

The courtiers had to obey the king.
So out they went. But they did not go far.
In a safe place, they sat down and
discussed what they could do.

"I know," said the fox after a while. "We shall make the camel *ask* to be eaten." And he told the others of his plan. They all agreed that it was good. And back they went to the king.

First the vulture stepped forward, bowing low. "Your Majesty," he said, "we have found no food. But we cannot let Your Majesty suffer. I am a poor creature. Eat me."

The fox pushed the vulture aside. "I have more meat on me!" he said. "Eat me, Your Majesty."

ow the leopard rushed forward. "I am not much good," he said, "but I could make a meal for the king."

he camel listened to all these offers and thought he must do as much. "Your Majesty," he said, "I, too, am willing to give away my life to save the life of the king. These old friends are more useful to you than I am. Eat me instead."

A t these words the fox, the leopard, and the vulture prepared to jump at the camel. This was what they were waiting for. But the lion stopped them. "You are all good and loyal subjects," he said. "My heart is touched by your offers, and I accept them all. I shall eat you in the order in which you offered yourselves."

he vulture, the fox, and the leopard were shocked. This did not suit them at all!

Away flew the vulture. Away ran
the fox and the leopard. And
they were never seen in that
part of the forest again.

The lion laughed
to see them go. Then he turned to the camel and
said, "You have been truly loyal and good. You shall be
my friend as long as we both shall live.
Now let us go through the forest and see if we can
find a meal for ourselves."
The camel was happy and grateful. And the lion
thought to himself, To be a king is good.
But to be kind is better.

The End